Dear Parents:

Congratulations! Your child is taking the first steps on an exciting journey. The destination? Independent reading!

STEP INTO READING® will help your child get there. The program offers five steps to reading success. Each step includes fun stories and colorful art or photographs. In addition to original fiction and books with favorite characters, there are Step into Reading Non-Fiction Readers, Phonics Readers and Boxed Sets, Sticker Readers, and Comic Readers—a complete literacy program with something to interest every child.

Learning to Read, Step by Step!

Ready to Read   Preschool–Kindergarten
• big type and easy words • rhyme and rhythm • picture clues
For children who know the alphabet and are eager to begin reading.

Reading with Help   Preschool–Grade 1
• basic vocabulary • short sentences • simple stories
For children who recognize familiar words and sound out new words with help.

Reading on Your Own   Grades 1–3
• engaging characters • easy-to-follow plots • popular topics
For children who are ready to read on their own.

Reading Paragraphs   Grades 2–3
• challenging vocabulary • short paragraphs • exciting stories
For newly independent readers who read simple sentences with confidence.

Ready for Chapters   Grades 2–4
• chapters • longer paragraphs • full-color art
For children who want to take the plunge into chapter books but still like colorful pictures.

STEP INTO READING® is designed to give every child a successful reading experience. The grade levels are only guides; children will progress through the steps at their own speed, developing confidence in their reading.

Remember, a lifetime love of reading starts with a single step!

Copyright © 2023 Disney Enterprises, Inc. and Pixar. All rights reserved. Published in the United States by Random House Children's Books, a division of Penguin Random House LLC, 1745 Broadway, New York, NY 10019, and in Canada by Penguin Random House Canada Limited, Toronto, in conjunction with Disney Enterprises, Inc.

Step into Reading, Random House, and the Random House colophon are registered trademarks of Penguin Random House LLC.

Visit us on the Web!
StepIntoReading.com
rhcbooks.com

Educators and librarians, for a variety of teaching tools, visit us at RHTeachersLibrarians.com

ISBN 978-0-7364-4369-2 (trade) — ISBN 978-0-7364-9037-5 (lib. bdg.)
ISBN 978-0-7364-4370-8 (ebook)

Printed in the United States of America

10 9 8 7 6 5 4 3 2

DISNEY · PIXAR

ELEMENTAL

A Family's Dream

adapted by Kathy McCullough

illustrated by the Disney Storybook Art Team

Random House 🏠 New York

Bernie and Cinder Lumen
travel to Element City.
They left their home
to follow their dreams.

Element City is filled with
Air, Earth, and Water people.
Bernie and Cinder are among
the first Fire people to move there.

Not long after they arrive,

their daughter, Ember, is born.

The family opens a shop.

Bernie dreams of passing

the shop on to Ember one day.

As Ember grows up, she wants
to make her dad proud.
But her temper often flares.
Bernie tells Ember that she will
be ready to run the shop
when she can control her anger.

One day, Bernie decides
to put Ember in charge of
a big sale at the shop.
Ember is thrilled!

But she gets upset
when all the customers
shout at her for help.
Her anger begins to spark.

Ember rushes down to the
basement to let off steam.
Her angry flames break a pipe,
and water gushes out!
A city inspector named Wade
washes in with the flood.

Wade cries when he has
to write tickets because
of the leak.
He feels bad that the
city will likely shut
down the shop.

Ember follows Wade to City Hall.
She tells him that closing the shop
would ruin her father's dream!
Wade is moved by Ember's story
and offers to help her.

He takes Ember to see Fern
in the ticket office.
But their plan does not work.
Fern sends the tickets to Wade's
boss, an Air person named Gale.

Wade and Ember find Gale

at an airball game.

They learn that the leak

in the shop is connected

to a bigger leak in the city.

Gale says if Ember and Wade
can find the source of the leak
and fix it, she will tear up the tickets
and not close the shop.

Ember and Wade find a broken
gate at one of the canals.
It is the source of the leak!
They push sandbags against
the gate, but the bags
are not strong enough.

At the beach, Ember and Wade
fill more sandbags.
Ember worries that her father's dream
will be ruined.
When her heat turns the sand
into glass, she has an idea!

Back at the canal,

Ember creates a beautiful

glass wall from the sand.

The leak stops!

She has saved Bernie's dream!

Wade is amazed by Ember's talent.

Wade invites Ember over
for dinner to meet his family.
After a glass pitcher breaks,
Ember makes it prettier.
Wade's mom thinks Ember
has a talent for glassmaking.

The family plays the Crying Game.

They try to make each other cry

with sweet and sad stories.

Wade is inspired to tell Ember

how much he cares about her.

A tear falls from Ember's eye.

Bernie announces that he is
ready to retire, and reveals
a new shop sign for Ember.
Ember is no longer sure
she wants to run the shop.
But the truth might hurt her father.

Ember tells Wade that she is taking
over her family's shop.
She cannot see him anymore because
Fire and Water do not mix.
But Wade thinks they should try.

He and Ember hold up their palms.

They are able to touch!

Ember does not know what to do.

How can she follow her heart

if it will upset her family?

Bernie throws a big party
for the opening of Ember's shop.
Wade shows up and shocks everyone
when he tells Ember that he loves her.

But Ember will not change her mind.
She cannot disappoint her father.
She tells Wade she does not
love him and orders him to go.

Suddenly, the glass wall
in the canal cracks.

Water rushes toward the city.

Ember tries to save the shop.

She is surprised and grateful
when Wade returns to help.
But the water is too strong.
They are pushed into the chimney.

Ember and Wade are trapped,
and the heat causes Wade to boil.
Ember tells Wade she loves him.
They touch as he turns into steam
and disappears.

Ember's parents find her.

She is heartbroken about Wade,

but she finally admits that

the shop is not her dream—

it is her father's dream.

Bernie says his *true* dream

is for Ember to be happy.

Just then, Ember hears crying,

and a drop of water

plops into a bucket below.

Was that Wade's tear?

Ember remembers the Crying Game

and tells more sad stories.

When Ember says she wants
to explore the world with Wade,
the bucket is filled with tears.
Wade returns!
He and Ember kiss.

Ember sets out on a new adventure!
Thanks to Wade and her parents,
she has learned to listen to her heart
and follow her dreams!